# Jack and the Beanstalk

Written by
Anita Loughrey

Illustrated by
Martin Remphrey

Jack lived with his Mum. They were very poor.
They had no more money to buy food,
so they were very hungry.

"Take Clara the cow to market, Jack,"
his mum said.
"You must sell her so that we have some money.
Then we can buy some food."

So Jack took their cow to market.
On the way he met an old man.
"Give me your cow," the old man said,
"and you can have these magic beans.
They will make you rich."
Jack was very happy and he took the beans.
Now he didn't have to walk all the way to market.

Jack ran home with the beans. He showed them to his mum. His mum was very cross.
"But they are magic beans," Jack said.
Jack's mum threw the beans out of the window.
"Now we have lost our cow. We have nothing," she said.

That night, as Jack and his mum slept, a beanstalk grew from the beans. It grew up, up, up until it was taller than the clouds.

The next morning, Jack woke up and saw the giant beanstalk outside his window. It was so big that it hid the sun from his room.
"I wonder what is at the top," Jack said.

So Jack climbed the beanstalk, up, up, up, all the way to the very top.

At the top of the beanstalk, Jack saw a big castle. He walked up to the castle and knocked on the door. Nobody opened the door.
But the castle door was open, so Jack crept inside.

Inside the castle, Jack heard loud footsteps.
Then he saw a huge giant.
"Fee-fi-fo-fum, I smell the blood of a little one!" the giant said.
Jack was very scared. He ran and hid in a huge cupboard.

The giant was carrying a hen. The hen looked small and sad in the giant's big hands.
The giant put the hen on the table and shouted, "Lay!"
Jack watched as the hen laid a golden egg.

Jack gasped. "A hen that lays golden eggs could make us rich," he said to himself.
Jack waited in the cupboard until the giant fell asleep. When the giant was snoring, Jack crept out of the cupboard. He grabbed the magic hen.

"Run! Run! Before the giant wakes up," cried the hen. Just then, the giant woke up.
Jack ran back to the beanstalk with the hen under his arm. The giant chased Jack and the hen.
The giant was angry.
"Fee-fi-fo-fum, I smell the blood of a little one!" the giant shouted.

Jack started to climb back down the beanstalk. He looked up. The giant was following him down the beanstalk!
Jack climbed down as quickly as he could.
At the bottom Jack jumped onto the ground.
Quickly he grabbed an axe and chopped down the beanstalk.

The beanstalk came down with a crash and the giant crashed down with the beanstalk.
The hen was happy. "You saved me from the giant," the hen said to Jack.

Jack showed the hen and her egg to his mum.
"It can lay golden eggs!" he told her.
"That's wonderful!" she said. "We can sell the eggs and we won't be hungry any more!"